PIRATE
Stew

Lou Carter
Nikki Dyson

ORCHARD

The bottle that lay on
the floor of the stream
Was home to a shrimp who
did nothing but **clean**.

SCRUBADUB'S HOUSE

Scrubadub **dusted** and **scoured** and **rubbed**.

SQUEEAAK

SPLOOSHH

SKRRITCH

He **tidied** and **swept** and he **scraped** and he **scrubbed**.

TAP TAP

And finally, when there was no more to do, He cleaned up the rest of the neighbourhood too . . .

He **polished** the crabs.
He **trimmed** all the reeds.

He **groomed** every frog
And **untangled** the weeds.

GASP!

He **shaved** all the catfish
And **lined up** the snails,

Then **shampooed** the fish from their heads to their tails.

Sea FOAM

SAY "SEA YOU LATER" TO DIRT!

Till one day a frog
rather bravely piped up,
"We're sick of this cleaning.
Enough is enough!"

"Enough!" said the crab.
"I don't mean to sound whiny
But creatures like me aren't
supposed to be **shiny**."

"**Enough**," said the catfish.
"Just look what you've done . . .
I'm meant to have whiskers and
now I have **none**."

Scrubadub left feeling terribly miffed . . .

"Let's see how they manage **without** me," he sniffed.

"I work **VERY** hard to keep everything neat.

I'm constantly rushed off my twenty-six feet.

They moan and they grumble—"But then he stopped dead . . .

SNIFF

...as **something**
came tumbling over
his head.

Swept from the ground, he was caught in a crate,
Dragged from the water and dumped on a plate.

All of his neighbours were lying there too,
About to be thrown in a **bubbling stew**.

The cook raised his knife and was ready to chop,
When all of a sudden the captain yelled . . .

"That crab be all **smooth** and that catfish be **weird**.
Shouldn't his chin have a **whiskery beard**?
Those **sparkling** fishes can't go in our broth.
This seafood be **dodgy**. I think they is **off!**"

With a sigh of relief, they were sent on their way,
But Scrubadub stayed – he had something to say.
"Just what have you pirates been up to?" he said,
With a tap of his foot and a shake of his head.
"This ship is **disgusting** – it's **filthy** and **grimy**.
Your treasure is **green** and your decking is **slimy**.

And as for you pirates,
you smell rather **whiffy**.
But I'll have you shipshape
and **clean** in a jiffy."

So he **polished** the floorboards,
And **shined** all the gold.

SCRUB SCRUB

SQUEAK SQUEAK

He **wiped away** bird poo,

SPLAT!

And **scraped off** the mould.

He **lined up** the rum,
He **washed** all the sails,

SHLOOP!

Then **scrubbed** every pirate

And **trimmed** all their nails.

SNIP!
SNIP!

"WOW!" said the captain. "It be like a dream!
Me ship and me crew be all **squeaky** and **clean**.
Me hair be all **soft** and me cutlass **ain't brown**.
Me trousers **don't crunch** when I goes to sit down."

"My work here is done," said the shrimp, full of glee.
He said his farewells and he jumped in the sea.

SPLOOSH!

Back home he was cheered by a welcoming crowd
And Scrubadub Shrimp felt exceedingly proud!

"YOU SAVED US!" said Crab. "If it wasn't for you,
We'd all have been cooked in that **potful of stew**.

And so we have built you a lovely surprise.

Just follow me . . .